SHORT STORIES
AND
VERSE

by
Jennifer Detlefsen

CONTENTS

The Bee and the Daisy

3

The Front Garden

The Mirror People

Peace

The Language of the Sea

The Secret of the Other World

The Wisdom of the Wind

The Young

2 Corinthians 13:11 *Be of one mind and live in Peace. And the God of love and peace will be with you.*

The bee and the daisy

One has a bright white face
One is stripey
Both need each other

A resonance is buzz buzz
Then the bee quickly appears
And hovers before sucking
sucking

The bright white daisy
flings it's head around
asking the slight wind for help
Bee Bee
smell my sweet Nectar

The enticing aroma
wafts through the air
floating on the sparse breeze

The small being returns
unable to resist the
enchantment

We will work together
My ally in springtime

3

Three

There were 3 medium
The sand was white
The sea was blue sandwiched in between
And the sky was pale gold

The lines were so finite
So sharp and defined
The white edge of sand
The blue waves behind
Then the sharpest straight line on the horizon
Where the sea and sky met

The eyes started there
And the pale golden sky
travelled back over my head
changing to azure where
the golden haze faded

White blue gold
Vast sand vast sea vast sky

The Master creates endless vista

The Front Garden

The young woman walked listlessly along the gravel on the edge of the road. She pushes the loose strands of her blonde hair out of her face annoyingly, and kicks small stones in her path every now and then.

She studies the gardens as she walks past, some quickly, because they were too unkempt to look at; others she peers at for a longer time, trying to figure out exactly what it is that makes them look so pleasant and inviting. Is it the neat rows of lavender, their purple heads bobbing in the breeze? And the perfectly sculptured circles of the box hedges, or the patronizing grandeur of the large heads of the roses? Is it the perfection of the manicured lawn, the stone figurines, the large round bird fountains with the water spilling over the edges excessively?

As she strolls by, not lingering long enough to attract any attention or unnecessary conversation, she imagines the kind of people who live behind these impressive facades.

They must be so perfect, she thought, just like their gardens. They'd have fabulous careers that took them all over the world, they'd have a large yacht where they'd spend their weekends, and they'd laugh all the time, while they drank expensive champagne and had interesting conversations about worldly matters.

The young woman heard the cry of a baby in the house down the road and knew she had to turn back. She changed direction reluctantly but as she did so caught a glimpse of a woman standing on the front porch of the grand home. They caught each others eye, and the young woman felt guiltily self conscious, as if the beautiful woman with the perfect suit and neat tied back hair, knew what she'd been thinking. She stroked her own untidy curls and wished she had spent more time trying to tame them today.

The woman on the porch suddenly smiled wistfully, and it was then that they recognized the mutual admiration in each others eyes. One saw in the other a life of wealth and ease, but she couldn't see the long hours worked or the constant pressure to sustain the public image and the desired lifestyle; the other saw a life of simplicity and the joy of laughing children, but she couldn't imagine the day to day struggle to survive.

The cries grew louder and the young woman brushed back her wispy hair as she hurried back . The rusty gate screeched on its hinge as she pushed it aside and she couldn't help but notice that hers was one of the overgrown and neglected gardens. The weeds pushed through dominantly, and the grass had grown unhampered for a long time. The yellow heads of the dandelions stood defiantly above the long stalks of grass.

She sighed in resignation, and smiled at the increasing volume of the child's lament, and went inside.

THE MIRROR PEOPLE

"Hi Sophie." Sophie smiled at herself in the large mirror on the dining room wall opposite the kitchen, as she plopped down her shopping on the benchtop.

"Hi Ben2." Ben didn't look in the mirror as he said it but he knew he was there reflected.

It was a silly little joke that Ben and his mum played every now and then when they got home. That their reflections in the mirror were real people; they looked just like Ben and Sophie but they had their own lives.

Ben was now twelve and they hardly ever played the game anymore but it was still fun now and then.

He walked over to the mirror and looked at Ben2.

"What you been doing Ben2?" He stared at himself and the reflection just stared back.

He moved his body from side to side and then waved his arms around. Ben2 did exactly the same. He poked his tongue out, and rolled his eyes.

"Mum! Ben2's copying me!"

"Well what do you expect him to do honey?"

"I dunno, he's so boring!"

And with that he picked up the controller and plonked himself in front of the tv.

"Do you have homework young man?"

"Yes mum." Ben answered sulkily and turned the tv back off.

"You can play once you've finished your homework." His mum kissed his head and ruffled his hair.

"I know, stop it!" He pushed his hair back and sat down at the table with his books.

"I'm going in the shower, make sure you finish it." Sophie was tired. As a single mum she was Mum, Dad and everything in between and her boss at work was particularly short tempered today. He was yelling at everyone, and insulting her, as well as the other workers, and although she let it slide at work, it played on her mind when she got home and tried to relax.

She liked her job of admin. on the computer but she definitely did not like her boss. He was a stupid arrogant old man, and she got sick of him trying to act half his age, making inappropriate comments to the women who worked for him. But it paid the bills and until she found something better, she would ignore him, and roll her eyes in unison with the other girls.

The water poured over her shoulders and soothingly down her body, and she turned the hot tap up a bit; finally she could relax. She breathed deeply and started washing her hair.

For some reason Ben couldn't concentrate. He wasn't doing that well at school, and for that reason his mother insisted he finish his homework every single night. It was no use arguing with her, she had him down pat; a sentence he'd heard a thousand times and hated to hear: homework or I get the controller, which is it? He couldn't win and gave up trying a long time ago. She could hide that controller in places you could never think of looking.

He scribbled bigger and bigger circles on the paper he was supposed to be writing on and then dropped the pencil on the floor when they got too big for the paper and went over the edge of the table.

He turned around and childishly pushed his nose against the mirror. When that hurt he stuck his tongue out and licked it. He watched his tongue licking the mirror and then looked at himself. He pulled his eyebrows up with his hands and opened his eyes wide. "Is that all you can do Ben2!" He was about to turn away when he thought he saw Ben2's eyebrow move. Had his eyebrow moved?

"Shit", he thought, "I hope I'm not one of those people who's faces twitch and they don't know it."

He peered closer and went to turn away, but there it was again. It moved, his eyebrow had moved! He was sure of it. Then his reflection bared it's teeth. "Oh shit, I'm going crazy!" "I haven't taken any drugs, what the hell!"

He looked in the mirror again but just saw himself doing nothing. "Oh good, I think I better lay off the sugar for a while, maybe mum's right about that stuff."

"Hey is that all you can do Ben?" The voice was sarcastic.

"Who said that?" Ben looked around the room but couldn't see anyone.

"Over here, dimwit." Ben2 flung his hand through the mirror and pushed Ben on the shoulder so that he nearly fell.

"What the hell!?" Ben had to grab the chair to stop him losing his balance and out of shock.

"Yeah you heard me, you dumbnut." Ben2 sneered through the mirror. "Is that all you can do, make faces at me? You look stupid." With that Ben2 let out a hearty laugh.

"What the hell!?" Ben couldn't speak and didn't really believe what he was seeing.

"Mum are you playing a trick on me? Not funny!"

Sophie walked into the room. She felt refreshed and was back on track. "Who are you talking to Ben? Put that phone away, and finish your homework." With that she walked back into her bedroom and continued getting dressed.

"You'll give me away you dumbnut."

"What the?!"

"Is that all you can say?"

Ben peered again at the mirror, yep that guy in there was talking to him.

"Are you friendly?" he asked.

"Are you?" Ben2 leant forward and his head and shoulders stuck out of the mirror until his face was close to Bens'.

"Look man, I'm sick of trying to copy those stupid faces you pull. Give it up ok?"

Ben stepped back and tripped over the chair. "Oh ok."

"They're not that stupid, they're funny." Ben gave a wry smile, remembering some of them, especially the one where he pulled his mouth down and his eye up.

"Believe me, they are not funny at all. Especially the one with the mouth and eye thing."
With that Ben2 moved out of the mirror completely, and walked around the room.

"Hey you can't do that!" Ben followed him.

"Why not? I do it all the time." He turned his head and raised his eyebrows mocking. "I play your games, I lie on your bed, I have a good time while you're slaving away at school all day." He laughed again and turned around to enjoy the indignant look on Ben's face.

"Liar." Ben sat down on the sofa. Was this really happening? This guy looked just like him, right down to the cool haircut and the loose laces.

"What are you?"

"Your reflection, dumbnut." Ben2 was picking up the controller.

"Who are you talking to Ben?" Sophie yelled from the other room.

"No one mum, it's the tv!" Ben yelled back.

Ben grabbed the controller from Ben2, but Ben2 just laughed. "I bet I can beat you on that."

"I'll bet you can't." Ben felt confused.

"Fine, I'll play you tomorrow after school, when your mum goes next door for a while."

"How do you know about that?"

"Don't worry about it, I know everything. And stop wearing that dorky tshirt, it's like a little kids one."

"This tshirt is cool!"

But Ben2 had already slipped back into the mirror.

Then he suddenly stuck his head out again. "And keep away from the mirror, I'm sick of pulling your stupid faces!" And he was gone.

Peace

The sun is shining
the sky is blue
A few white clouds
move slowly across the view.

Today is still
for once I blend in
I am unremarkable in the landscape
As blending as a tree or a bird.

I do not have to move
or do anything
Or notice anything

I just am
A moment of peace

THE LANGUAGE OF THE SEA

As I walk along the beach
I watch as sea meets sky,
sealing the horizon.

At the end of the earth
the seagulls soar above the calm expanse,
hovering in the blowing wind,
the same wind that claws at my clothes
It's creeping fingers forcing through the weave
Causing me to pull my coat
tight around me.

My thoughts envelope the scenes
seeming to blend in with this timeless atmosphere;
drawing them out and across the vast water
as if no knowledge was to be held back

The waves lapped at the shore
skimming along the surface of the sand,
hungrily trying to crawl up the land.
They whispered to me, jestingly,
knowing I could not perceive or understand
the strange language they thrust out,
to anyone who might be listening.

They told of far away places
and hidden secrets,
tales and stories
and the mysterious workings of the heavens and universe

If only we had ears to hear
then we would know
all the answers.

The Secret of the Other World

The setting sun was silent on the horizon, reflecting her mood. She sat, motionless, staring out at the great expanse of sea before her, the blue endless water touching the blue endless sky; she wondered what might lay at the other side. If she swam and kept on swimming, would she come to a world that was different; a world that held exciting adventures just waiting to be lived? Or a world that would be even harder than this one, where you tried and tried but still your tears drowned your heart?

She shivered at the thought and decided that it would be a totally different world on the other side – a world that was full of happiness and laughter and you never knew what interesting things were going to happen next.

She peered at the disappearing edge of the sun, the searing yellow globe turning the blue sky to brilliant orange, and as it dropped over the edge of the blue distant line, she realised the other world was too far to swim.

She walked leisurely towards the rowing boat moored to the miniature jetty, that sat on the water bobbing as if in anticipation, and got in. She untied the rope from the offending pole and began rowing, unconsciously heading towards the spot where the sun had lingered, and then dropped.

The old man sat still, his back leaning heavily against the stone wall of the yacht club building, empty now, except for the echoes of the days sport. He had watched her, a young girl gazing intently, dreamily, out at the horizon, and knew that she would take his boat.

So, as she pupposefully strode acros the sand and then began rowing into the purple sky until she became a black silhouette, smaller and smaller, he did not try to stop her.

Instead he sat, an invisible observer, as still as the quiet beach; but his sharp eyes followed her, until the black spot lingered, llike the sun had done, and then vanished at the same place.

The young girl worked the oars expertly, and with strong plunges bore them deeply into the water, as if she'd been doing it all her life. Her arms did not not tire lilke they should have, and she only felt elated that some strange power had overcome her and drew her, pulled her, in a direction completely new and unknown . She did not give a thought to what she might be leaving; she felt only a release, a sense of freedom, and a touch of tension, patient, as the feel of a revelation, about to be revealed.

She did not know how long she'd been rowing, but it did not matter; her objective was sure and she would go to this new place, aware that she would find something that would surpass anything she had ever seen before.

As her boat leaned and seemed to slide down a slope, she saw the sun again, and felt it warm on her skin. It momentarily blinded her, and then she stepped out into a rainbow of colours.

The boy ran onto the beach and looked around frantically, searching for something, or someone, with his dog close behind.

The dog bit at his heels playfully, as if unaware of his masters anxiety. The boy ran from one end of the foreshore to the other, and then stopped and sat down on the pier, his shoul ders slumping.

The old man saw him and guessed who he must be looking for. The boy was tall for his

age, but as he came closer he didn't look as young as he had at first. A young face, the old man thought, but older eyes. Young eyes that had already seen too much. This world was not good to the young, he knew.

The dog licked at the boys fingers trying to attract his attention but after a while gave up and ran, barking excitedly at some seagulls, scattering them.

The boy got up and kicked the sand dejectedly, and then again harder, shooting particles into the crisp air. "She's not here", he thought, looking at the glorious sunset. "No one here but an old man!"
"Damn!" he said aloud, not caring if the old man heard.

But the old man was not listening. He was just sitting there, staring at the line where the end of the ocean met the darkening hues of the sky.

- - - - - - - - - - - - - - - - - - -

cont.......

It was early. The azure sky welcomed the morning sun and the air was already warm. It was the middle of summer and even in the early hours the cool water shimmered, threatening, but never succeeding, in cooling the hot days.

The boy was up and decided to try the beach once more. After all, she always came here if something was troubling her. He did not run this time, but walked slowly, and was not surprised when he found the beach empty. It was still early. As he turned the corner of the yacht house though, he came upon the old man, sitting in the same place he had been the evening before. Had he been there all night, he wondered, and passed him by.

The old man saw the girl coming and saw the light shining in her eyes, from a long way off. He watched her tie the boat to the pier, exactly the way he had tied it the day before, and then walk toward him, but he did not see her pick up an object from the bottom of the boat and take it with her.

The girl had never seen the old man before but she walked straight up to him, and smiling, gave him the thing she was holding. His own eyes reflected for a moment the light in hers, and then he looked down at what she'd placed in his weathered, wrinkly hands.

On a quiet beach, in the early morning, a dog barked in happy recognition, and a boy ran in the direction of a girl stooping over an old man.

He wanted to ask her where she'd been and why was she talking to an old man? He thought he'd seen her give him something, but he wasn't sure. Ah, what did it matter? She was back and he was relieved. He looked into her eyes and saw something strange there, something new. But when he saw her smile, he remembered how glad he was to see her. He decided he liked the new look in her eyes, as if she was wiser, or older, and he hugged her laughing. They walked away together, happy, the dog running ahead.

And when the girl looked back, the boat was gone. And so was the old man.

THE END.

The Wisdom of the Wind

Life was as full as chirping birds in a green tree.

But suddenly all the birds flew away; and the leaves turned brown.
The wind whistled through the empty boughs as if singing a song of sojourn.

But it's wisdom was without knowledge.

Worse was to come.

The black clouds gathered overhead and their bellow rang across the earth;
for all the world to hear.
The storm was bold and the rain pelted down, driven by a rage, primitive, and
ferocious in its awakening. The lightning flashed relentlessly, exposing the tree
in its despair, without mercy.

But there was.

The storm moved on and the thunder rolled no more.

The clouds disappeared to reveal an azure sky.
The sun arose and spread its warming fingers over the tree's branches;
caressing it's trunk, seeping into its roots and filling it with life and love.

The tree burst into glory, with proud magnificence, and smiled its new buds up at
the blazing entity.
The flowing river beneath reflected its shining leaves, and the birds were attracted
by its lustrous foliage and splendour.

The wind returned, this time meekly, and the tree sang to it a song of
eternity.

The Young

The young are superb
They have fair skin
I look at them
and realise I don't look like that anymore

The young own the world
It is there for their taking
But we are just hanging on
to the glory of what we used to be

I struggle with the thought
That all my battles have been won or lost
they're over
too old to know the joy of something new
to admit that everything
the Youth create is better

Faster, cheaper, smoother, affluent

My eyes can't sparkle like they did
when I was Young

Because the promise of good things is gone
Just like my Youth

www.ingramcontent.com/pod-product-compliance
Lightning Source LLC
Chambersburg PA
CBHW041031170626
46815CB00001B/47